I0445365

DRILLING THE MAID

DIRTY BILLIONAIRE BOSS

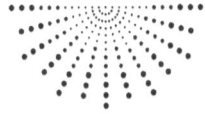

TALA MELTON

plicit Press
Erotica Fiction

GET NAUGHTY UPDATES

Click here or Visit
TalaMelton.com
for more Naughty Maid Stories

Drilling The Maid: Dirty Billionaire Boss

Digital Edition 1 is Copyright © 2020 by Tala Melton. All rights reserved.

No part of this publication may be replicated, redistributed, or given away in any form without the prior written consent of the author/publisher or the terms relayed to you herein. This book contains adult material and scenes of a graphic and adult nature, and some profanity which some may find offensive. All characters are 18 or over.

eISBN: 978-1-62327-710-9

Print ISBN: 978-1-62327-711-6

CHAPTER ONE

"*Y*ou do know that this breaks every rule..." Tina said to her boss as the private jet landed in Abu Dabi.

"It doesn't. They're usually surrounded by many beautiful women, so what difference does it make that I too bring my own *beautiful* woman?"

Logan Chambers was the kind of man who really thought the rules didn't apply to him. He was aware of the rules, mind you. He had to be. One didn't become as wealthy as he was without knowing the rules, and without knowing which ones could be bent or broken to suit his purposes.

"Yes, Sir, I know. But usually, these women aren't *a part* of the negotiations. They're just there to pour drinks and hand out pens..."

"I'm disappointed at how you view the Arabian women... *Tisk Tisk*!" Logan teased.

"You know what I mean," Tina defended herself.

"I do... You're just my cultural attaché... We all know how destructive I can be when left to my own devices. So you coming along is a *good thing*!"

"I'd rather be making your bed," Tina said, a whisper to herself mostly.

They sat silently in the Range Rover that met them at the airport. They had a long drive into the desert, where a luxury tented camp would be their home for the next couple of days. *When in Dubai,* Logan had teased Tina when he asked her to accompany him.

The desert was beautiful, the sunset playing a massive role in the epic pictures unfolding over every dune. There was a lot of sand a lot. Logan was face deep in an iPad, checking and responding to emails. He really never stopped. Tina was snapping pictures of the beautiful scenery that really wasn't just brown dunes and wind. The colors were really kaleidoscopic.

"So what's the plan again," Tina asked Logan when he finally stopped with the email.

"No plan, really. You're just here to guide my steps and make sure I don't offend before the deal is signed!"

"Me being here is offensive," she pointed out. Logan his himself in the tablet again, a huge *knowing* smile on his face.

The tent camp appeared in the distance, quite like a mirage. The sun was just setting, the fires around the camp already ablaze, the synthetic lighting making the presence of generators obvious. The tents were beautiful. The white flaps flowing in the early evening breeze made the whole scene look like the epitome of an *Arabian Night*. Tina wasn't quite sold on the tent camp idea, regardless of how many times Logan had used the word *luxury*, but now, seeing it up close, she was.

"Huh... What did I tell you?" Logan said, proud of himself for organizing this himself.

"Yes, yes... It'll do!" is all Tina said. She had an incredible poker face, helped by the wrap-around her head, a sign of respect, a requirement, in fact, for *all* Arabian women.

His tent was magnificent. She wondered at the incredible effort it must have taken to set this up. Just her tent was a three-division monstrosity. A sitting area upon entry, followed by a large bedroom, with an ensuite bathroom for good measure, with an actual bathtub. There was no plumbing, really, but the alternatives were luxurious and more than acceptable. The bath would require, as Tina found out upon arrival, seven large pitchers of hot water to fill.

She lay in the beautiful tub, a pre-dinner soak, and she was lost. The wind was a constant feature, so that it was now an acceptable accomplice to this experience. Even the sand played along, blowing away from them so that they could, in the now night, appreciate the shapes as it danced across the surface of the expanse.

"Is your room acceptable," Logan asked Tina when they sat down under a *set up for this purpose* gazebo to dinner.

"Stop it now; you did good, okay... Get over it... Get over you!"

They were really extremely comfortable with each other. There was a 20 year age gap between them, but Logan was extremely personable, extremely approachable. He was a nice guy, through and through, and this was why he was so successful. He made everybody comfortable around him, comfortable with him so that it was easy for anybody to do whatever he asked them to do.

Dinner was a feast of flavors. Very few of them were familiar, the instruction to the Arabic chef hired to keep them fed was to surprise them, and to keep it local. Logan had extraordinarily adventurous tastebuds, Tina, not so much. But she too enjoyed the dinner, even when she was told pre-main meal that the meat was a camel. She tried it, she liked it, and so their first dinner went off without any real upsets.

"So, I'll see you tomorrow..." Tina said, wanting to try out her new bed now.

"Let's make it good; a lot is riding on this..."

CHAPTER TWO

*T*here was a moment's apprehension before they entered the penthouse boardroom with a panoramic view of the city. Three sides of the massive room were glass, and the view stretched to ocean and desert. Skyscrapers dotted the spaces in between so that it looked like a city from science fiction. This Arabic city made no sense. It also made perfect sense.

"This is Tina Billings," Logan introduced her, adding when he remembered, "My cultural attaché!"

She looked perfectly respectable; her head wrapped, her face uncovered though. She knew that as a Westerner, this was allowed, but only just. Her skirt wasn't as short as it might have been back in the States. *Just* below the knee, it revealed incredible calves that ended in *just* too high stilettos.

Tina kept her eyes low, not making direct eye contact with the men who felt obliged to shake her hand because she had extended it. Also, they were wary of offending Logan, an American connection that was essential to this deal, even though none of them would say this to him directly. Tina actually did everything perfectly to protocol. She was so respectful, in fact, of the men and their culture the by the time they broke for lunch, she was guiding the meeting, leading it almost. The four Sheiks were really enamored, and more than just a little impressed.

"It's going better than we expected," Muhammed Al Jafar said to her. He was incredibly handsome so that Tina couldn't look into his piercing gray eyes. They were quite mesmerizing, hypnotic almost so that Tina knew that to look at him directly would be the end of her.

"It is," she said, before adding," he's behaving himself!" She was looking at Logan, who was chatting to the other three *closer to his age* men.

"He does seem *calmer*..." Muhammed said, also looking at Logan so as not to put pressure on the *raven-haired* beauty to look at him directly. "I think bringing you along was a very good idea!"

Tina nodded in his direction, acknowledgment, thanks. Muhammed was watching her in his periphery. She really was breathtaking. The four men across the room watched her, too, Logan pointing in her *general direction,* making it obvious that he was discussing her or explaining something of which she must have been an integral part. Tina pretended not to see.

The second half of the meeting was as successful. There was a clear avoidance of Tina this time, just because decisions were now being made. She was more comfortable with this, actually, so that even though every man's eyes were still on her, rather obviously, she didn't mind being the *welcome distraction* that Logan had intended. When the final folders were opened, ready, and waiting for final signatures, every detail was confirmed and sorted. I's and It's dotted and crossed; the folders passed from gentleman to gentleman, thousand-dollar pens putting million and billion-dollar signatures to paper.

"A celebratory dinner," Muhammed Muhammed said when they were well and truly done with the meeting. He was speaking to Tina directly now, and she was again caught in that delicate, no direct eye contact dance from earlier. This man, older, was almost as attractive as Al Jafar.

The convoy left directly for the tented camp; instructions were already given to the chef to prepare something special for the new number of guests. Logan had, as a courtesy, extended the dinner invitation to the wives of his new Middle Eastern partners, but all of them made various versions of the *short notice* excuse for their wives. They obviously wanted to *engage* with Tina uninterrupted. Logan and the beauty would be leaving tomorrow, so this night was really all they had.

It was interesting for them to engage with a woman who had a world view beyond the Arab world. And that she had an intimate understanding of their world made her all the more alluring. They were all taken by her, quite completely. All of them religiously faithful to their wives, they entertained only in their heads what interesting bedroom talk they might have had with her if this was a possibility. Muhammed Al Jafar entertained the most carnal thoughts but respectfully kept these to himself.

"You would have a very bad influence on our wives," Mustafah said as they sat smoking a post-dinner *hookah*.

"Very, very bad," both Muhammeds reiterated.

"And we get the real reason why they were not allowed to come," Logan said.

"You have it wrong, Logan... Nobody *allows* Arabic women to do anything. They're extremely strong-willed... The best we hope for on any given day is that they agree with what we *suggest*.."

"And to think the first world still has a draconian view of

7

the woman of Arabia," Tina said, looking at Logan. The three guests looked at Logan, too, accusingly.

"I was wrong, okay, I'll admit!" Logan apologized without apologizing, looking at Tina with *you'll pay for this* look.

They chatted until well into the night. It was just after 1 AM when the guests departed, having said their goodbyes. The flight out the next morning would be an early one, and so the inconvenience of a more formal goodbye was unnecessary. Tina said goodbye to Muhammed Al Jafar last, this time losing herself in the grey lakes that were his eyes, even more, devilish when lighted by moon and fire.

The two Range Rovers disappeared into the desert, the headlights visible for a very long time, though. Logan and Tina stood there watching the lights appear when atop a dune, and disappear when they drove down the far side of them. And then they were gone. Still, just for a moment, the pair stood in the night, under a million stars, watching the pitch-black night.

Then Logan was watching Tina. When she turned to look at him, he looked away. Again, when Tina's eyes were in the darkness, his eyes fell back on her. He watched her closely now, searching, admiring.

"What," she asked without turning to look at him.

"Nothing," he said, turning away from her again.

Then he was watching her again. He shook his head and chuckled. Now she turned to look at him.

"Okay, what is it," she asked, really wanting to know.

"You're really something else; you know that," he said after a moment, still shaking his head, still chuckling.

"Oh, I know..." she said, before turning and walking to her tent.

CHAPTER THREE

*T*ina sat in the front of her tent; the side panels rolled up so that she could enjoy the night sky. The Arabian night was really quite a showoff. She watched as her tub was filled by two men whose job it was to fill it, no matter the time of day or night. 'I hope they're paid well,' she thought, knowing that they would be, of course, Logan excessively generous.

She poured herself some jasmine tea and thought about the day. It had actually been more successful than she'd imagined it would be, and at the risk of sounding *'braggy'* or arrogant, she had to acknowledge the part she had played in the day's proceedings. Tina sipped her tea, enjoying what really was *her* moment.

"You can do so much better than tea," Logan said, appearing quite suddenly out of the darkness.

"Your disrespect knows no bounds," she teased, looking at the bottle of something in his hand. He lifted the vodka, looked at it, shrugged.

"I won't tell if you won't," he said, coming and sitting next to her. He took two tiny teacups from the tray, and after looking around like a naughty child scared he'd be discovered, he poured the cups quite full of the clear spirits.

The silver teacups *dinned* slightly when they were brought together, a toast to the day. Then they both took very measured sips of the liquid with a forty-three percentage. It was strong; it was smooth; it was every contradictory thing an expensive bottle of vodka should be.

"Ouch..." Tina said.

"It will taste better soon..." Logan promised. In the absence of a suitable mixer, the vodka really was quite harsh. And since it was almost 2 AM, going to try and find a mix in the makeshift kitchen was out of the question.

They sipped the vodka slowly, carefully. They tried in vain to convince themselves that each subsequent sip tasted better. It really didn't.

However, no sooner had they just made it through the cup, and Logan was pouring them another. It was too late for Tina to object. So she just took a deep breath and took the cup when it was handed to her.

"It's not getting any better," she said.

"I know, the last one," Logan said, surprising himself by drinking the whole contents of his teacup in one swig. He was looking at Tina again, really looking at her. This wasn't admiration, though, not anymore. It was something else.

She watched him too, sipping slowly on her own cup, noticing this changed look in his eyes. She knew what it was. She'd seen it many times before, not from him, but from other men. She'd seen it this evening in Muhammed Al Jafar's *sober* eyes. She smiled inside, taking the complement.

Without explanation, Logan moved into her suddenly, taking the cup from her and sending it down his throat. Then he put a hand under her skirt and kissed her as suddenly, directly on her lips. He kissed her in that way that let her know that he needed to get it out of his system. That it had been a long time is coming, and she needed to let him get it out. It wasn't a bad kiss either, so she let him. She was actually kissing him back, even though she didn't feel that she was.

His hand went between her legs quickly. Logan was seizing the moment before sense returned, to him, but more especially to Tina. They had always been closer than a boss, and his employee should be, but there had also never been anything sexual about it. If Logan had ever looked at her that way before, he had never said anything, never shown anything.

Tina had certainly never seen him as anything but her *maybe just a little bit too fun* boss!

"Are you sure this is a good idea," she asked, Logan's finger under her panties already, already searching for and finding her entrance.

"Please..." he said, sending the finger fully into her.

She was hot; she was wet; she was just right and *tight*. He kept his finger inside her, not moving, his mouth back on hers to stop Ber from speaking. Tina had always been very sensible, and this was the last thing he needed her to be now. She had really impressed him today, much more then she had before, and he was out of ways to thank her. This was, in his mind, the best way to thank both of them, the best way to end what was a brilliant day.

Tina knew that this could be bad for their professional relationship. She also knew that it could be good, too, provided they were both mature about it. She really hoped as she kissed him back now, that the latter would be the case. She really liked her job, and she was more than a little fond of her boss.

"Wait," she said, easing the finger out of her. She threw her eyes at the opened panels so that Logan knew that she felt a little exposed. One did get the impression that they were being watched, if not by the night, but by people you couldn't see because of it.

He stood up and let her gather herself before standing. She walked into her bedroom, protected and private, so that she felt a little more comfortable. Logan came up behind her and held her against him. His erection rubbed against her, filling out completely. He was grinding his meat against her as he moved them towards the elaborate bed. She got on it and turned onto her back as Logan, still standing, got undressed completely.

She took her skirt off, and then her shirt. Logan got onto the bed and helped her with her bra. He pulled her panties down slowly; his eyes fixed on where she was neatly and quite cleanly shaven. Logan dropped the panties on the bed and put his nose between her legs. He took a very deep breath.

Then his tongue moved over her. He licked her over and over again, enjoying the taste of her immensely. When his tongue went inside her, she was the one breathing deep. She inhaled hard as his tongue moved deep, making contact with every part of her inside. It was out of her briefly so that he could inhale her scent himself, and then it was back inside her, determined that she would weep from her secret place quite quickly.

He was kissing her on her belly suddenly; his tongue replaced again by just one finger. He was moving his finger now, in and out of her, as his mouth made it to her perfect mounds. She really had the most incredible breasts, and Logan showed his appreciation by sucking tenderly on her nipples.

She was Cummings now so that the sentence she had

started was interrupted. Logan kept his finger moving inside her until she had reached her peak and come completely down to earth. His finger moved inside her long after. When their mouths met, they kissed for a long while, the finger still firmly in place.

CHAPTER FOUR

*L*ogan pushed Tina further up on the bed, still on top of her. He wasn't kissing her now, just looking at her. Tina, too was looking at him, unsure of what to do. The moment was strange, almost awkward.

"What else can you do," he asked.

"I don't know... Whatever it takes, I guess.."

"Ain't that the truth..." he said, parting her legs with himself. He was rubbing his hardness against the outside of Tina. She ached for him inside her now, despite her recent orgasm. Or perhaps because of it.

She moved herself up on the bed just a little more, so that his erection was pointed directly to where she needed him to be. Logan made no move for it, though, moving himself higher on the bed too so that again they were rubbing up against each other, much to her frustration.

He smiled and closed his eyes. Logan was just teasing her, wanting her to want him before he let her have him. He needed to be sure that this wasn't one-sided, and this was the only way he could think of to be sure. Now that he was, though, now that he knew she longed for him, he was ready to let her have it.

Logan had been ready for quite a while, actually.

"Please," she said now, mimicking him unexpectedly. How quickly the tables had turned. How quickly the hunter proved himself, the prey begging to be devoured.

He didn't answer her, not with his mouth anyway. He just started to go inside her with his firm fullness, forcing her legs apart just that much more as he made steady progress inside her. It wasn't long before all of him had settled deep, taking up all the space she had. In fact, it created two or three centimeters just so that his entry was full and complete.

"There we go... There... We... Go!" He said this over and over as he started to move out and then in, out and then in, completely both ways. His eyes were on this movement in and out of her. She took him easier than he had thought she would, and he was glad there was no struggle. He knew that he wouldn't have been able to handle not getting inside her quickly, such was his desire for her.

Tina just lay there, half sitting actually, her eyes closed, as over and over Logan fed himself into her...

After the longest time, he pulled himself from her. She was surprised so that she opened her eyes to see what was wrong. Logan said nothing, pulling her down further on the bed so that she was on her back properly. He went inside her again, deeper it seemed now just because she wasn't in a half running away position, a position he himself had put her in. He fed himself into her harder now, enjoying the fullness of his entry in this new, more comfortable position. Logan checked her face once before closing his eyes and delivering a stroke after sensually slow stroke into her until she started to quake.

She literally shook under him, something he hadn't experienced in a very long time. This was his *thing*, in his younger days. He'd always had the ability to make women shudder and shake. But he hadn't been able to do this in a while.

Logan really appreciated this reminder of just who the hell he was, who he had always been...

He rolled onto his back, Tina on top of him, flat, her breasts on his chest. He didn't want her to straddle him, just wanted her to be as comfortable as possible. He expected no effort from her, wanting to be well and truly in charge of everything that happened to her and with her. She really deserved it.

Logan put his hands on her back and held her tightly against him. He fed himself as fully to her from below. He moved his pelvis in long movements, pushing his butt into the mattress to increase the distance for his penetration, and also the intensity. Tina's legs fell on either side of Logan so as to receive him easier, deeper.

His hands moved down her back and onto her butt. He pushed her down into himself as he fed himself into her a little more. Over and over, all of him was inside her; Tina held firmly in place on him by Logan's large hands.

Again he was rolling them over so that again he was on top of her. He placed a hand under each of her thighs and parted her legs wide. He was really going for it now, giving her all that he had in him and then some. She was looking at where their bodies met now, not believing the sheer intensity of this penetration.

"I think this was a very good idea..." Logan whispered in her ear.

'It was,' she thought, unable to say it though.

They fused together perfectly, Tina's legs held in a perfect split by Logan's grip. He really was holding her quite tight, pushing her legs apart quite hard. She let herself be moved; however, he wanted, enjoying the control he had of her. Tina had never thought of him this way, really she hadn't so that this whole experience was new and thrilling.

He gave himself to her a little more, bringing her close before he pulled himself from her completely again. This was really quite a phenomenal experience, and he was determined to make it last.

Logan was between her thighs again with his mouth, kissing her gently at first before aggressively licking and tonguing her. His tongue went in full and filled her quite completely, not as completely as he had with his generous erection, but for what it was, it was epic..

Again he brought her close, close enough to make her shudder again. She was convulsing, and he had to hold her down with both his hands, his grip firm. He moved his tongue inside her a minute and then removed it. Then his tongue was inside her again before it was out. He seemed to enjoy the sensual seizures she was having because he kept her just out of reach of her orgasm.

Logan came up to her face for the third or fourth time now, inserting two fingers inside her as he did. He didn't move these fingers, just lodging them inside her to give her something to work her body against as she brought herself down from the tremors. He didn't know what else to do.

"Are you okay," he asked when she stopped shaking.

"I think so," she said before she burst out laughing.

He asked her what it was with just his eyes, just the look on his face.

"How the hell do you do that," she asked.

He moved his fingers in and out of her now, working his mouth down her belly and back on to her quivering mound. With just his mouth, just his tongue, he brought her to shuddering again before he said, a smile on his face, " Just like that!"

CHAPTER FIVE

*T*ina lay on her back, touching herself and not. Her hands moved over her own body as he went to pour them another teacup of vodka. This wasn't so much because he wanted it, or because she wanted it, but just because he knew that she needed a bit of a break. He also needed a minute because he was getting a little too hot.

They both downed the teacup in a single gulp. Then Logan came up behind her on the bed, both of them on their knees. He rubbed his still hard self on her ass cheeks and against her lower back.

She moved her legs apart and lifted herself on the bed. Logan tucked himself underneath her, from the back, and then guided himself into her front. With each stroke, he lifted her up and off the bed slightly. He tried to dig himself deeper into the mattress so that there was a little less lift, but this just wasn't possible.

He lifted her off the bed for half a dozen strokes. Then he got to a dozen, and then two. Then he himself was too close, so he stopped, and pulled himself from her. She leaned forward and lay on her stomach, opening her legs and raising her ass, an open invitation he couldn't ignore.

Logan was inside her again, on top of her fully, thrusting deep into her, trying to control each stroke. But suddenly, he was passed the point of no return, hitting her hard in this position, unable to hold himself back any longer. She didn't mind, wanting him to cum now.

He lay on her and in her. His weight was a little much, but not uncomfortable. They lay that way for a long time before he pulled himself from her and fell on his back. She didn't move for a minute until she had sufficiently recovered, turning to put her face in his crotch and her mouth on his meat. She was sucking on him slowly, no real intention, just because she really liked to suck soft cock.

"You're starting something," he said to her, still flaccid. She thought he was just being a man, arrogance making him make promises he couldn't possibly make good on. He was just saying what he thought she needed to hear.

But then he was hard again, and Tina looked at him, surprised. It hadn't been ten minutes, and the middle-aged billionaire was ready to go again. And he wasn't about to settle for just her mouth on him, knowing himself, knowing that she could suck on him for days and he wouldn't cum.

He'd always been that way. While he enjoyed the feeling of a mouth on him, no mouth was ever able to bring him to climax. He didn't expect Tina to do any different. He didn't want to frustrate her, knowing that she would think that it was her, and it really wasn't. It was all him.

He let her suck on him for a minute longer, and then he pulled her up to him. She got on top of him and eased him into herself, their eyes locked. There was something about the way she moved herself up and down on him that made him watch with intrigue where their bodies fused again.

Logan had no idea what was happening inside her, but whatever it was she was doing, he didn't want her to stop.

"How..." he asked.

"How what?"

"How the hell are you doing that..."

He watched her move on him. She was going up and down, up and down, and then in deep circles. Her hands were on her own breasts as she just moved using nothing but the muscles in her legs and her thighs. She was really more powerful than he thought she was, and it was easy for Logan to relax and let himself be taken by a *Wonder Woman*.

"Yes," he said.

"Yes," she said.

She moved over him like a woman possessed now, her eyes on him still. There was nothing about this that had anything to do with Logan now, for the moment. She was bringing herself to another orgasm and expected orgasm, an intended orgasm. She exhaled hard and leaned forward so that her mouth met his.

Logan turned them so that he was on top of her now, again. He had to get himself over, much like she just had, with a sort of *selfishness* that was necessary. He pushed himself into her over and over again until he was spilling himself onto her. It was quick, too quick, but there was nothing to it. He needed to cum, and now he had.

They sat in the tent, the room hotter than it was earlier, so that she wished that the side panels of the tent were lifted. They weren't, though, and they were unable to move, so she went to the bathroom and rolled up the panel on the side-wall, possibly because of the design.

She looked at the tub, full. It was incredibly inviting, and after shouting her intention into the room to Logan, who she thought had passed out now, and she slipped into the bathtub. The water wasn't hot, but it wasn't cold. She sank to the bottom of the deep tub and lay there, taking a minute.

A moment later, Logan was getting into the tub behind her. She moved to make space for him and then lay with her back on his chest. They had nothing to say to each other. No words were necessary. They both knew that this meant nothing, except maybe that it had opened up a new aspect to their relationship, one where they would, if they wanted to, help each other out.

Logan did fall asleep for a while, and Tina just lay there. She enjoyed the water on her and over her, and she actually enjoyed the sound of him snoring, happy that she had done this to him. He might be a billionaire during the day. He could be a billionaire at night. But for a few hours, they were just a man and a woman, and she had defeated him.

He had defeated her, too, she knew. Her finger on herself, she knew that she was a little sore, even though she had to admit to herself that she still wanted more. She moved herself against his softness, not quite an attempt to resurrect it, but not an attempt to do the same.

Tina lay back and allowed herself to fall asleep, hoping that when they woke up, probably when the water was too cold for them to be in it, that he might want to go again. She really hoped that he would.

"Do you want to get out," he asked suddenly, his eyes still closed.

"No, it cool. This is nice," she responded, closing her eyes.

They lay there for the longest time, falling asleep in shifts and then together. None of them made a move to get out of the tub, so they relaxed into it, despite the hour, despite the water getting colder than was comfortable. There was no rush to do anything, and they figured they could sleep properly on the plane...

ABOUT THE AUTHOR

Tala Melton is an emerging erotica author of naughty maids and their billionaire bosses.

Readers: I want to expand a few of the stories to see where the characters can be explored further. If there are any of the stories that you would like to read more about again, I'd love to hear from you!

Visit my blog at Tala Melton Blog
Join my newsletter for free exclusive previews Tala Melton Newsletter
Follow me on Twitter at Tala Melton Twitter
Like my page on Facebook at Tala Melton FB

Sign up for Free Stories from Xplicit Press Authors
Xplicit Press Updates
Like Xplicit Press on Facebook
Follow Xplicit Press on Twitter

MORE NAUGHTY MAID STORIES BY TALA MELTON

Naughy Maids and The Dirty Billionaire Bosses

www.ingramcontent.com/pod-product-compliance
Lightning Source LLC
Chambersburg PA
CBHW020815130626

46554CB00006B/2448